First published in 1996 by Sapling,
an imprint of Boxtree Ltd, Broadwall House,
21 Broadwall, London SE1 9PL
Copyright © Geoffrey Planer, 1996

10 9 8 7 6 5 4 3 2 1

Reproduction by SX Composing DTP
Printed and bound in Great Britain by Cambus Litho Ltd.

ISBN: 0 7522 2335 6

A CIP catalogue entry for this book
is available from the British Library.

MOUSE TALES

Mrs Fizackerly's Little List

Geoffrey Planer

■ sapling

For James and Rupe
and Ollie

'They've all brushed their teeth and tails and
they're all ready for bed,' shouted Mrs Tail
from the kitchen as soon as Mr Tail
had shut the front door.
'Right, then, off we go to bed.
Small Tails and tall Tails –
Up, two, three,' said Mr Tail.
'Into bed at once, Jack,' said Mr Tail.
'Quick march. Chop-chop. Come along,
what's the matter with you, Jack?'
'My name's not Jack, it's Jeff,' explained Jeffrey.
'Ah,' said Mr Tail, with just a
twitch of his whiskers,
'I'll forget my own name next.
And that reminds me of a story

Another Night,
Another Mouse,
Another Tale . . .

Mrs Fizackerly's
Little List

Mrs Fizackerly had five children.
She also had a dog and a cat, a flock
of sheep, two pigs and a goat.

And a cow that wouldn't moo.
And a car that would. And a husband.
And a family. And a grumpy daughter
who never laughed.

And shopping
that needed
to be bought,

and food that
needed to be
cooked,

and clothes
that needed
to be washed,

and gardens
that needed
to be weeded

and ... always so, so much to do.
One day Mrs Fizackerly got up extra,
extra early to try and get everything
done. She took out her pencil and pad
to write a list of important things to do.
'First things first,' she thought to herself,

and pencilled
in the words
at the top of
the paper:
'Get Noona
to cheer up.'

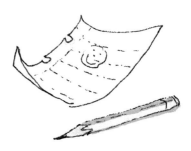

Then she
couldn't
remember
the next thing
to do, so she
decided to
go and get
the milk.

She put on Mr Fizackerly's jacket
over her nightie, put the pencil behind
her ear and went outside.

The milk wasn't there.

But she knew that the flowers needed
watering, so she took an empty milk bottle
and went round to the front of the house,
picking up Ericajane's cowboy hat,
lost the day before, on the way.

As she passed by, Mrs Fizackerly noticed a huge bunch of dandelions growing outside Fizzy's bedroom window. She was pulling them out when her eye fell on one of Noona's red wellington boots which had been left out all night.

She tucked it under her other arm
and then noticed that the paint on the
window frame was peeling like anything.

She remembered that there was a brush
and some old paint in the shed.

So, putting the weeds in her jacket pocket, she went and filled up the milk bottle with white paint. The window was open and she stepped inside to get at the frame,

but as she did so, she saw that Fizzy's potty needed emptying.

She took off her slipper so that she could put the boot on her foot, then put the slipper in her mouth and picked up the potty.

Mrs Fizackerly was trying to remember
why she was there when she noticed
that the pantry door was open.
'Porridge,' she said to herself. She put
the paintbrush behind her other ear,

balanced
the packet
of porridge
on top of
the potty

and was heading
back into the
kitchen when
she saw that
Billy's hamster
had escaped
and was sitting
on the floor.

She scooped it up with her free hand
and, since she couldn't put it anywhere
else, she popped it down the
red wellie for safekeeping.

It did mean that she had to hop so she
wouldn't squash it, though.

Noona came into the kitchen for
breakfast, looking grumpy as usual.
She smiled a bit, though, when she saw
her mother hopping at the stove wearing
Dad's tweed jacket and a cowboy hat.

She tried to
stop a giggle
when she saw
the paintbrush
behind her
mother's ear –
it had splodged
her hair white –
and the slipper
in her mouth.
She started
to laugh and
laugh when
she saw
the hamster
peeping out
from the boot.

She screamed
helplessly as
she watched
her mother
pour porridge
into the potty
and put it on
the cooker, stirring
it with the pencil from behind
her ear. And when Mrs Fizackerly
poured the white paint
from the milk
bottle into the
potty too,
Noona felt
she would
explode.

Mrs Fizackerly looked up.
She looked round. She looked down.
She remembered her list:
'Get Noona to cheer up'.

Mrs Fizackerly started to laugh and the
slipper fell out of her mouth into the potty

She laughed and laughed.
Noona laughed and laughed and laughed.

They both laughed till the tears rolled
down their cheeks. Mrs Fizackerly reached
into her pocket for a handkerchief and
then wiped her eyes dry with
the bunch of dandelions.

Even the hamster laughed then.

'How could anyone be so silly, eh?'
said Mr Tail. 'At least she did keep smiling,
eh, John?' he added as he marched his
365 little Tails off upstairs to bed.
'Now then – brushed teeth?'
'Yes.'
'Brushed Tails?'
'Yes.'
'Brushed whiskers?'
'Yes.'
'Good night everyone. Good night,
Jimmy … er, Jeffrey,' said Mr Tail.
'Good night, Auntie.'
'Hrumph,' said Mr Tail, and he
went downstairs for supper.

Small Tales,
Tall Tales,
Bedtime -
for All Tails